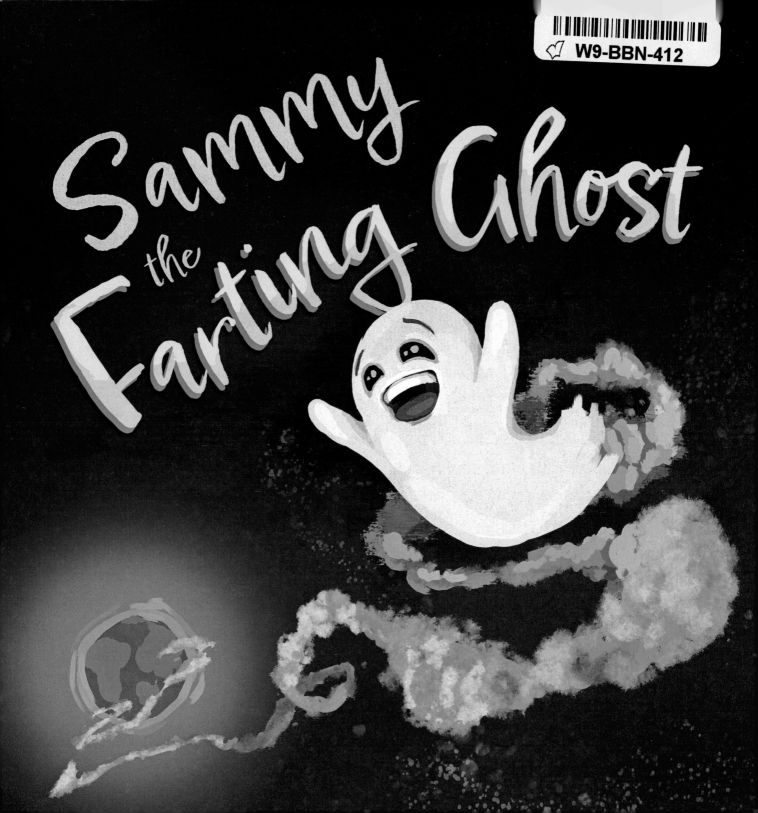

Sammy the Farting Ghost

Spooky Sammy was happy and hoppy, quick and cute,

but his tummy often rumbled
his bottom did toot

it blared like a trumpet

and whistled like a flute.

He practiced all year,
flying and hopping,

But farted and pooted
and honked without stopping:

he hopped and he flew
with bombs
always dropping.

What shall I do? he thought,
To whom shall I turn?
What'll calm my belly
when it starts to churn,

or stop the booms
that my backsides burn?

He asked the Witch
what would his tooting tail control,

and she said, "Potion in your tummy!
That's your goal.

It'll calm even the biggest whale's blow hole!"

Sammy tried
the Witch's Potion
but it tasted like glue.

He said "I'll never drink Potion the way that you do!

I only eat candies, sweets, and chocolates, too!"

So Sammy explained
to the werewolf
all of his woes

"Chasing cats," he said,
"'s the best cure-all a
werewolf knows!

You won't have time
for what your bum blows!"

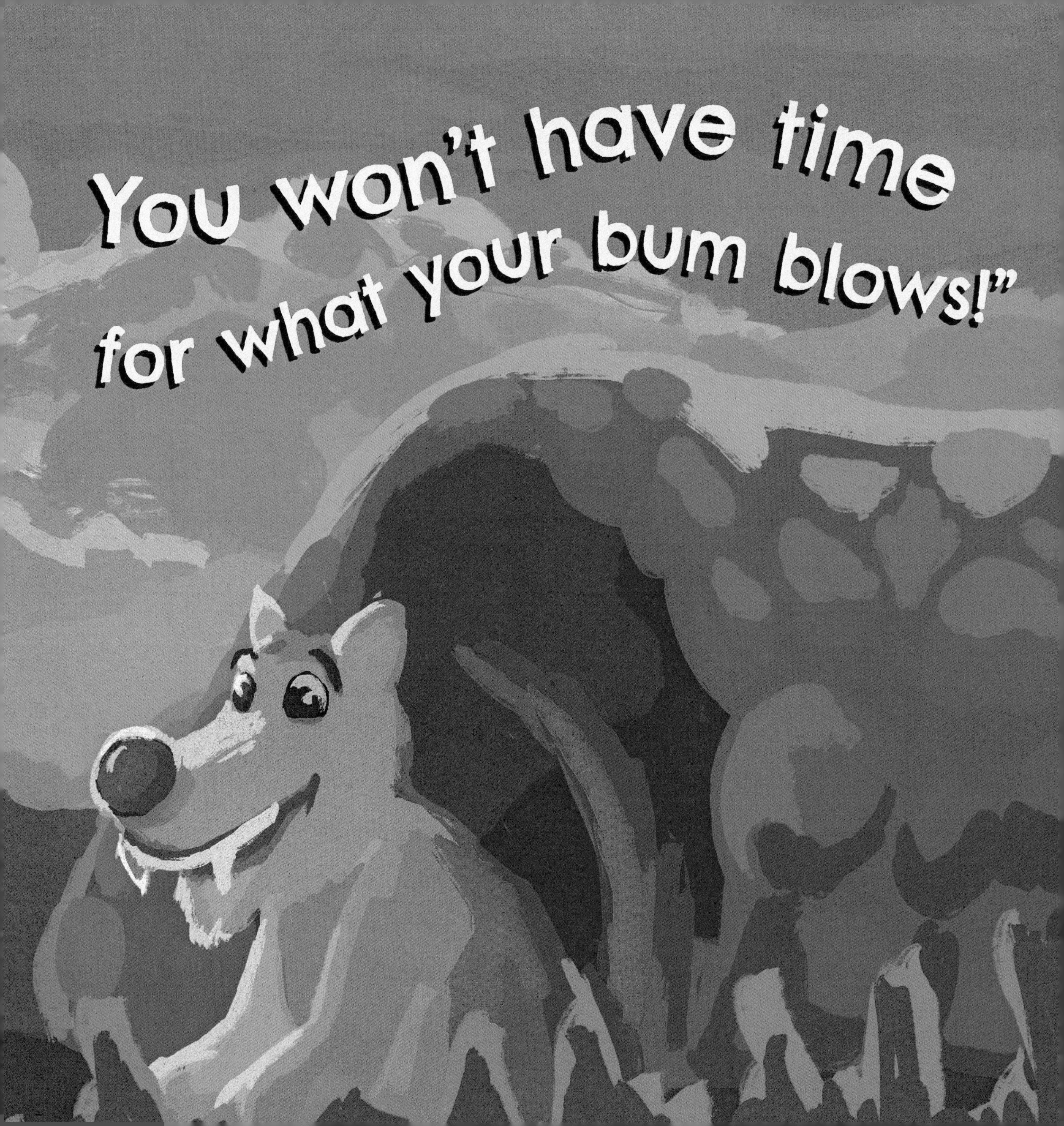

So Sammy chased a cat
but at the end of its paws,

the cat also had, he learned,
very sharp claws.

The Sammy hopped to the mummy, pooting all the way,

who heard Sammy's problem and opened his mouth to say,

"Sit still, close your eyes,

Sammy tried it,
but his bottom
had a big surprise:

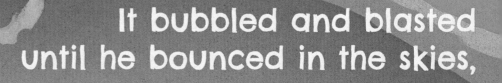

It bubbled and blasted
until he bounced in the skies,

encircled by clouds

and squadrons of flies!

Next, he tried
to plead
with a stone

to help get his gas
to leave him alone.

But the stone was sleeping, and spoke not a groan.

Spooky Sammy pouted,
hands hung low, feeling blue
What can I do? he thought.

What to do?

His Mom came
and told his sadness

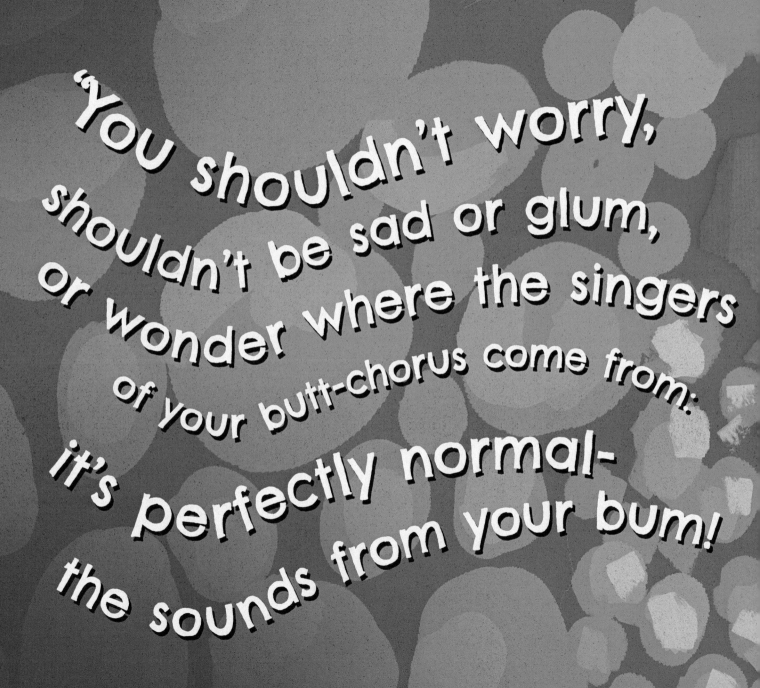

For ghosts of special,
Halloween spooky stock,

have always been able to
squeak, squeal and squawk.

Farting's the secret
that makes us

Normal ghosts can't find the world's sweets in a night,

and make one's face shine bright with light.

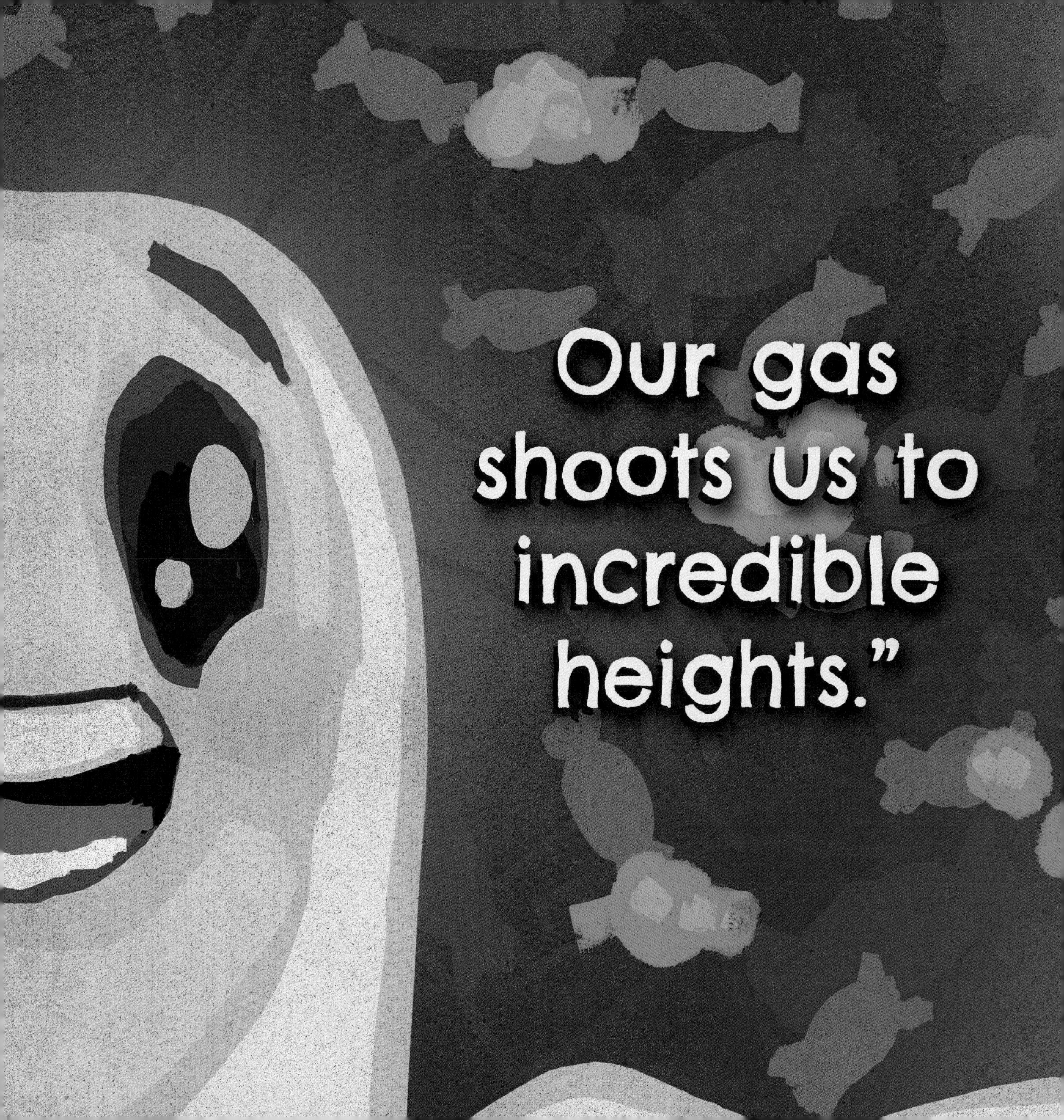

Our gas shoots us to incredible heights."

Now Sammy
the World's greatest Ghost
His jet-powered bum blasts
shoot him everywhere,

From Łódź to La Paz
to Trafalgar Square.

Made in United States
North Haven, CT
07 October 2022

25167530R00018